Roasted Peanuts

Tim Egan

HOUGHTON MIFFLIN COMPANY

BOSTON 2006

For Margaret

www.houghtonmifflinbooks.com

The text of this book is set in Horley Old Style.
The illustrations are ink and watercolor on paper.

Library of Congress Cataloging-in-Publication Data
Egan, Tim.
Roasted peanuts / written and illustrated by Tim Egan.
    p. cm.
Summary: Sam the horse gets picked to be on the local baseball team, but unfortunately his friend
Jackson the cat, despite being a good thrower, is not selected.
ISBN 0-618-33718-0 (hardcover)
[1. Baseball—Fiction. 2. Friendship—Fiction. 3. Horses—Fiction. 4. Cats—Fiction.] I. Title.
PZ7.E2815Roa 2006   [E]—dc22   2005004950

ISBN-13: 978-0618-33718-7

Printed in Singapore
TWP 10 9 8 7 6 5 4 3 2 1

Of all the things that Sam and Jackson loved, nothing beat baseball. Nothing was better than a warm afternoon at Grant's Field, with the sun shining on the bright green grass, the cheers of the crowd, and a bag of roasted peanuts. Nothing.

As far back as they could remember, the two of them had always played ball together.

Sam was an amazing athlete. He was very strong and fast, and most folks assumed that one day he'd play for the big leagues.

Jackson was another story.

One might expect him to be quick and agile, but that wasn't the case. He was the slowest cat anyone had ever seen. He couldn't hit the ball if he tried, and he rarely caught it, even when it was thrown right to him.

He did, however, have a terrific arm. He could throw really far and with great accuracy, and Sam, being a good friend, always encouraged him.

"Another great throw," he'd say. "You're a natural, Jackson."

Jackson would smile and say, "Yeah. You and me, Sammy. We're gonna be legends."

Now the day came when Sam and Jackson were finally old enough to try out for the local team, the Grazers.

All through the tryouts, Sam was incredible. He hit almost every pitch out of the park and caught every ball that came near him. It was obvious who the best player on the field was.

It was also pretty obvious who the worst was.

Although he threw the ball well, Jackson didn't throw fast enough to be a pitcher. He never even came close to hitting a ball, let alone catching one, and he ran so slowly that some folks actually started laughing.

It was a tough day for Jackson, and he went home feeling very defeated.

When the team was announced the following week, it came as no surprise that Sam was chosen and Jackson wasn't. As they read the names, Jackson said quietly, "Well, at least one of us will be a legend."

It kind of took all the joy out of the whole thing for Sam.

Practices started soon after that, and while Sam was gone every day, Jackson spent much of his time sitting on the steps of his apartment, feeling sorry for himself. Sam practiced hard with the team, but without Jackson around, it just wasn't as fun.

One afternoon after practice, Sam noticed a poster on the wall of the ballpark. He tore the poster down and ran over to Jackson's apartment.

"Check this out!" he shouted as he held up the poster. It read, "WANTED. PEANUT VENDOR. MUST THROW WELL. FREE ADMISSION TO EVERY GRAZER GAME."

"It's a sign!" shouted Sam.

"I can see that," said Jackson.

"No," said Sam, "it's a sign for you! You throw great! You could come to every game!"

Jackson looked at the poster. "Thanks, Sammy, but no thanks," he said.

The Grazers had their first game the following Saturday, and, to everyone's surprise, Sam played terribly. He struck out every time and dropped three fly balls. The Grazers lost, 17–3.

Many in the crowd blamed Sam.

Sam smiled, turned toward the pitcher, and dug in his shoes.

The pitcher threw the ball and Sam knocked it out of the park.

The crowd went crazy.

As Sam rounded the bases, a lady yelled, "Hey, peanut guy, over here!"
The lady was a few sections away and Jackson didn't feel like walking
that far, so he just threw the bag of peanuts.

It landed perfectly on her lap.

"Wow," said a fellow, "did you see that throw? Hey, how 'bout a bag

up here!" This guy was at the top of the bleachers. Jackson pulled back and threw another bag and, again, it landed right on the guy's lap.

"Amazing!" shouted someone else. Jackson kept throwing the peanuts so perfectly that by the fifth inning the crowd was watching him as much as the game.

As the season continued, Sam played brilliantly and the Grazers started winning every game. And with each game, Jackson became more well known himself. It became a tradition to let him get really far away before yelling, "Hey, Jackson. Over here!"

His record was an unbelievable sixty-three rows away.

Sometimes, after the games, Sam and Jackson would stand together outside the park and sign autographs.

The season came down to the final game on October 26. The Grazers were in top form, but the other team, the Barkers, were also very good. In the bottom of the ninth inning, the score was tied, 7–7.

There were two outs with a cow on third, and Sam was at bat. He swung at
the first pitch and missed. As the crowd moaned, a lady yelled, "Hey, Jackson,
over here!" Jackson turned and looked. She was at least a hundred rows away,
and he didn't think he could make a throw that far.

The pitcher threw the second pitch. Strike two.

The crowd started grumbling as the lady shouted again: "Jackson. Come on!
Over here!"

"Nobody could make a throw that far," yelled someone, "not even Jackson."

Jackson looked down at Sam. Sam looked up at Jackson.

By now, some of the players on the field were starting to look up at the stands.

The pitcher threw the third pitch just as Jackson threw his bag of peanuts. Sam swung at the ball and hit it perfectly. As the ball sailed over the field, the peanuts sailed over the crowd. Some folks weren't sure which one to watch. The peanuts landed perfectly on the lady's lap and the crowd went crazy. Unfortunately, Sam's hit was dropping into centerfield. It would be an easy out.

But the guy playing centerfield had been so busy watching Jackson's throw that the ball hit him on the head and the cow on third base ran home and scored the winning run.

Rarely, in the history of baseball, has a crowd gone so wild.

Sam became a champion and played for seven great seasons. He still goes to the games every Saturday, where he watches his best friend break his peanut-throwing record every year.

And everyone agrees that, while many legends have come and gone at Grant's field, only one is still part of the game.

The Looking Book

BY P. K. Hallinan

ILLUSTRATED BY Patrice Barton

ideals children's books
Nashville, Tennessee

ISBN-13: 978-0-8249-5607-3

Published by Ideals Children's Books
An imprint of Ideals Publications
A Guideposts Company
Nashville, Tennessee
www.idealsbooks.com

Text copyright © 2009 by P. K. Hallinan
Art copyright © 2009 by Patrice Barton

Color separations by Precision Color Graphics, Franklin, Wisconsin
Printed and bound in Italy

Library of Congress CIP data on file

10 9 8 7 6 5 4 3 2 1

Designed by Eve DeGrie

For Jerry ~ P.B.

"**Turn off that T.V.!**" Mommy said one day.

"Go on outside . . . go outside and play!"

"We're watching cartoons," Kenny said with a pout.
And Mikey chimed in,
    "We don't want to go out!"

But Mommy just smiled
    through their long, sad sighs;
and when they were done,
    she held out
        a surprise.

A very strange surprise . . .

"What are they?" asked Kenny,
taking hold of his prize.
"Do I fold them or bounce them
or put them on my eyes?"

"They're lookers," said Mommy, as plain as can be.
"They help you to look and they help you to see.

"So go on outside; go out the back door.
And look with your lookers
     like never before."

So out the back door to the wide-open spaces
they marched with their lookers in place on their faces.

It didn't take long to find something to see.
Within only moments, Mikey found a great tree.

"It's wide and it's tall, and the leaves are all green.
Why, this is the best tree that I've ever seen!"

Then they looked at each other and smiled in kind
and decided to see just what else they could find.

So they both went out looking . . .

Kenny sat down
    on a small patch of ground
and parted the grass
    that grew all around.

"This grass is amazing!" he joyfully said.
"There are all kinds of things here—
brown, yellow, and red!

"There are twig-things and rock-things
and dirt-things and string-things,
along with a whole lot of little black bug-things!"

And Mikey added . . .

"There are bunches of bugs
    going every-which way!
They don't sing or dance,
    but they know how to play!"

Then he reached down and picked up an old wooden stick
and yelled out to Kenny, **"You better come quick!**

"There's a ladybug here on this piece of wet wood.
She's not wearing a bow tie or funny red hood,
but she's crawling along like a ladybug should—
and really much better than a cartoon bug would!"

But Kenny was too busy to come . . .

He sat by a rosebush smelling a rose,
holding the flower right under his nose.

He sniffed it and whiffed it
and let out a sigh,
then fell on the lawn
with a breathless "Oh, my!"

"**Look!**" Mikey yelled, pointing up at the sky.
"**An honest-to-goodness, real-life butterfly!**"

"**I just don't believe it!**"
Kenny said suddenly.
"**There's so much to look at
and so much to see!**"

They looked high.

They looked low.

They looked very hard!

They looked with their lookers
all over the yard.

It wasn't till later,
        when dinner was cooking,
that Kenny and Mikey
        finally stopped looking.

With lookers in hand
        and eyes big and round,
they went in the house
        to tell what they'd found.

They said,

"There were tree-things
and bee-things
and roses
and weeds . . .

small things
and tall things
and flowers with seeds . . .

there were all kinds of new things,
green, purple, and blue things . . .

"There was so much to look at," they said with a shout,
"that first thing tomorrow, we're going back out!"

They gave their lookers back to Mommy
and said . . .

"You want to know something,
the best part of all?
You don't need the lookers—
don't need them at all!

"Yes, that's the best thing,

the best thing about them . . .

you don't have to wear them—
you can see things without them!"